For Suzie

Good reading....

Lizzy Strathan

The Extraordinary Magics of

Emma McDade

Libby Hathorn

For Suzanne Edith

Illustrated by Maya

Melbourne
Oxford University Press
Oxford   Auckland

No one need ever have known about the three magics of Emma McDade. No one outside her family or school friends or the people in her neighbourhood, that is. They had all known about Emma's magic powers since she was quite a little girl. But then something very dramatic happened which brought TV cameras and newspaper reporters to her door. And that was the end of keeping the three magics of Emma McDade a secret.

By the 6 o'clock news the whole city knew and half the country as well. And by midnight people all over the world had heard about the three extraordinary magics of Emma McDade. By morning Emma had invitations to visit the United States to be interviewed on Good Morning America, and then go on to Hollywood and sign up for a movie. Next day there were invitations from other countries around the world. The hot dry countries were particularly insistent that she come at once.

There was simply no peace for Emma and her family after that. The phone and doorbell rang, mobs of reporters came to the door, and groups of people simply waited about on the offchance that Emma might emerge from her house and do one of her magics.

Her parents said, 'Perhaps we should all go into hiding until this blows over.' But they decided that as Emma's face was now so well known there'd be no getting away with something as simple as that.

Now just how Emma got into this situation is quite a story.

Emma McDade was mostly an ordinary, everyday little girl. During the week she lived an ordinary, everyday kind of life. Emma went to school and played with her friends in the yard, ate a cheese and tomato or sometimes salami and lettuce sandwich for lunch, and walked home with her best friend

Phyllis every day. On weekends she went to Phyllis's house to muck around, or they met at the local swimming pool or at the local picture theatre if a good movie was on. If there wasn't a good movie on they'd hire a video and watch it at Phyllis's, or sometimes they'd skateboard on the steep hill outside Phyllis's house. Other times she stayed at home and played with Charles and James, the two small boys next door on one side, or the cute little baby Nia, who lived on the other side. She babysat for Nia's Mum, too, and would make a few dollars to buy stickers and crazy pens.

Emma *seemed* ordinary and everyday. But the truth was that she wasn't ordinary at all. Emma was an *extraordinary* little girl because of the magics. As Emma changed from a chubby baby into a sturdy toddler and then into a schoolgirl, her parents discovered things about her that didn't exactly add up to *ordinary* and *everyday* and *normal* any more.

For one thing they found out that Emma was strong. Not just strong. Or very strong. But exceptionally super strong! She was as strong as Samson had been when he'd pushed down the pillars of the temple with his bare hands. One day, when she was two and a half, she lifted up a heavy wardrobe in her bedroom with the greatest of ease. She'd lost her dummy underneath it and her plump little hand couldn't reach to grasp it. Her mum was amazed when she went into the bedroom to investigate the noise. There was her little daughter lifting the wardrobe as if it were a matchbox.

Her dad came running when he heard. 'Well I never,' he said. 'Look at that. A child of her size lifting a great lumbering old wardrobe! I should know exactly how heavy it is because it took three of us to move it. Three of us! And she's lifting it with one hand, too. She could be a weight-lifting champion if we get her some dumbells! Clever little thing! Must take after my side of the family, Bub.'

(He always called Emma's mother Bub even though her name was Coral.)

But when Emma's parents had recovered from the surprise of her super strength they decided they weren't so keen about the dumbells. Emma should be the one to decide about being a weight-lifting champion, when she was a bit older.

'We'd better not tell a soul about Emma's extraordinary strength,' they'd said to each other, 'or there'll be a great big fuss and the TV cameras and newspaper reporters will want to barge into the house, and Emma's life will be a misery. She won't have a normal childhood at all. We won't tell anyone. And we won't ask Emma to use her magic strength, ever.'

But they did.

Sometimes when Mum or Dad were working round the house they just couldn't resist asking Emma, 'Would you just carry the piano upstairs, love?' Or, 'Could you just carry this rock in the bush garden from here to here?'

Of course they never asked her to do these things when there were others around, but the kids in the neighbourhood found out anyway, and they would ask Emma to do things too.

'Could you lift up this telephone box for a moment to see if my money rolled under it?' Or, 'Emma, there's an enormous Council dumpbin outside our house and Mum doesn't want it there. She says it makes our house look untidy. Could you put it down on the corner? Oh, thank you so much!'

But then there was the second magic too, which Emma discovered when she was at pre-school. Emma's friend Arna Lupos had been taught to whistle by her brother and she was showing off like mad to all the kids in the yard at pre-school.

'Bet you can't do this,' she said to this kid and to that one. '*Wheeee wheeee,*' and she'd whistle loudly. The others pursed their lips just like Arna had. They'd blow and blow and go red in the face. Sometimes one of them would make the faintest little sound, but mostly they couldn't do it at all. Arna would whistle again for them, only louder and longer this time.

Emma practised whistling for hours at home. Next day she sat with Arna all morning and by lunchtime she could make a little faint *eeeee,* and alone in the bathroom she could go *wheeee* quite softly.

It was the next day at home after she'd practised some more, and could whistle quite as loudly as Arna, that it happened. She was in the sandpit again and she began to whistle. Oh louder and louder it went, and she was quite surprised because it had a high sweet ring that resounded in her ears. However the truly extraordinary thing was that Emma's whistle brought the birds down out of the sky!

One minute she was sitting alone in the sandpit, and the next thing there were tens, no hundreds of birds all flocking into the garden where they sat enchanted by Emma's long piercing whistle.

She tried out the new magic at pre-school and most of the children loved it. But the teachers were not so keen. Every time Emma whistled with the long high piercing sound tens and then hundreds of birds would flock down into the playground, squeezing in beside one another all over the asphalt and the seats not to mention the heads and the shoulders of all the kids. They would leave a frightful mess behind; there'd be droppings everywhere.

Finally Mrs Head told Emma and her dad (when he came to pick her up in the afternoon) that Emma was not to whistle like that any more. Mrs Head said she did love birds, she really did. But oh the mess made by so many birds in such a small space!

'You can do it at home as much as you like, pet. You can be a friend to the birds like St Francis of Assisi, and whistle away to your heart's content. But not at pre-school. It's too — well, too *surprising*, Emma. So no more birds out of the sky at pre-school, okay?'

Emma didn't like the way Mrs Head finished with the *okay* because it wasn't a question really, but what could she do but agree to Mrs Head's request? Mrs Head was the Head after all.

The third magic of Emma McDade wasn't discovered until Emma went to big school. The kids there who had been at pre-school knew about the bird magic and the strength of Samson, but everyone, including Emma, was very surprised by the weather magic.

One lunchtime, Hugh, Christine, Arna, Phyllis and Emma were playing follow-my-leader on the hill in the playground behind the school. When Hugh jumped up on the seat and balanced on one foot, Christine, Arna, Phyllis and Emma all copied him. When Hugh curled himself up in a ball and rolled down the hill at top speed, they all followed and ended up in a laughing heap at the bottom. And when Hugh put out his arms and twirled around and around on the spot, everyone else immediately did the same.

But when Hugh went hopping across the playground on his left leg, Christine, Arna, Phyllis and Emma didn't follow him.

They didn't follow because they were too busy watching Emma still whirling and twirling, faster and faster until her face was a pale blur.

Almost immediately there was a crack of lightning and a roll of thunder across the heavens, and the rain came down in great heavy splotches. Oh it was a storm and a half!

Phyllis cried out to Emma, 'You made the rain come, Emma. You made the storm. You did!'

'Rubbish,' said Hugh who had come back to shelter with them under an awning. He was angry with Emma for spoiling the game. He felt a fool because he'd hopped clear across the playground before he'd realized no one was following. No one had been interested in the fact that he'd been doing star jumps by the canteen, except a big boy who'd leaned down awfully close to his face and had said so quietly it had made Hugh's blood run cold, 'Get real, why doncha?'

Hugh looked around and saw the other kids watching the twirling whirling Emma, and then the storm broke over his head with a great shattering sound.

'It's just a storm that was coming anyway, Phyllis,' Hugh yelled at her through the drumming rain. 'Emma didn't have anything to do with it.' He looked at the sheets of heavy water all around and added, 'If she did, she can darn well stop it then because we're all soaking.'

Arna glared at him, 'Oh, what would you know, dumbo.'

'I know it's nothing to do with Emma,' he insisted.

But of course it was. It was her third magic! The next day she tried the whirling and twirling almost privately in her backyard. Charles and James were watching fascinated through a hole in the fence as she whirled around.

'What's she doing?' whispered James. 'Is she sending for cats or dogs?' He had seen the bird magic a number of times and thought that Emma was awfully magical whatever she did.

There was the sudden overture of thunder and lightning that made the two behind the fence jump in fright. And then the full music of the heavy drumming rain sent the children on both sides of the fence indoors.

Emma, nodding her wet head soberly as she ran across the garden, said to herself, 'I thought as much. It's weather magic.'

'Well, it's sure raining cats and dogs now,' said Charles from behind the fence pulling his little brother towards their back door.

'It is not!' James said disgustedly. 'It's only raining water!'

'It's like Noah's flood!' said Mum, bringing in the two little lovebirds from the back verandah, and rescuing the two kittens still mewing in surprise.

Emma didn't tell anyone much about the third magic. Arna and Phyllis had guessed at once, but Emma knew the weather

magic was going to be big trouble. She only used it once at
school when Phyllis had begged and begged her to bring up a
storm so she and Arna and Abdul and Sylvia wouldn't have to
go out and pick up papers in the playground as punishment for
being in a noisy fight in the corridor before school. A teacher
had said crossly that they were making 'a disgusting row' and
that they were 'acting like hooligans' and that they could
'jolly well go and clean up the playground at lunchtime
and learn a lesson!'.

Emma did the weather magic to rescue Phyllis and the
others who simply loathed picking up papers. Phyllis knew this
particular teacher would forget all about the punishment by
the next day. She had given Emma a Mars Bar in return, and
had promised to tell no one, absolutely no one, about the
weather magic.

So Emma had nearly forgotten about the third magic herself, and practically never used the second or the first either, when the bank robbers came to town. They were hopeless bank robbers and desperate ones. They came into the main street in a very beaten-up car with stockings over their heads.

While shopping, Mrs Azzarpardi noticed the dinted car with ALIANT in big silver letters across the front. She noticed the V was missing because she knew it should read VALIANT. She also noticed that the driver and the passenger were wearing stockings on their heads.

'Strange,' she said thinking about it while she did her supermarket shopping. 'And they were right outside the bank.' She took five tins of spaghetti in barbecue sauce instead of her customary one because she was so deep in thought. 'Stockings on head, outside a bank, a beat-up old car. I wonder if it could mean . . .' She decided to tell the local police.

By the time Mrs Azzarpardi had wheeled her shopping trolley down the main road to the police station, the bank robbers had robbed the bank, jumped into the ALIANT and were heading across town. It didn't take the police long to track them down because Mrs Azzarpardi had given such a good description of the car, and, even though the robbers no longer had stockings over their heads, the police recognized the desperadoes at once.

'After them!' said Officer MacDonald when she first spotted the beaten-up car. The police car, siren wailing, set off in hot pursuit.

The ALIANT was an old but souped-up number and could go fast. Oh it made a valiant attempt at escape, swinging round corners at great speed, doubling back and darting off in unexpected directions. The police car had trouble trailing this dextrously handled heap of a car and lost it after the first few

streets. But Officer MacDonald knew her stuff and anticipated just where the robbers would be heading.

'Turn around now!' she said to the surprised Officer Gilbert, for turning around set them in the direction of the park. Sure enough, they caught sight of the old wreck heading for the thick foliage and the track through the park. The police siren wailed a greeting at the old ALIANT.

The robbers knew they'd had it now, for there was only one straight road out of that suburb and the police would tail them and nail them for sure. So they decided to abandon their faithful steed, and hide out somewhere for a while, hoping the police would get tired of waiting around.

'We'll grab the money and run,' said the long, thin, anxious one to his small mate.

'Good idea,' said the short, fat one grabbing the money bags from the back seat where they'd been flung.

It was really bad luck for the 452 kids and 15 teachers that the robbers chose to stop right outside their primary school. With their bags of money clutched in their hands, they dashed across the playground and into the first doorway they could see. It was the great iron door of the canteen with its bars and shutters. The robbers battened down the shutters and clanged down the bars. Feeling safe and sound, for the time being anyway, they made themselves huge peanut butter sandwiches. They were now very hungry.

Meanwhile Officer MacDonald had asked for reinforcements on the two-way radio, and then borrowed a loudspeaker from Miss Myers the Head.

'This is Police Officer MacDonald speaking,' she said slowly and clearly and oh-so-loudly. 'Do not panic, children and teachers. I repeat, do not panic.' All the kids and teachers jumped in fright.

'You will be perfectly all right if you do as I say. Two bank robbers are hiding in the canteen. I would like everyone to leave the building at once and go home while we apprehend them.'

'What's *apprehend them*?' asked Arna as she walked quickly down the stairwell with all the other kids from 3J and 4M.

'It means *nick them*,' said Hugh. 'Everyone knows that.'

'All right, smarty pants. Everyone. Did you know that, Phyllis?'

'Sort of,' said Phyllis, 'but I wonder how they'll nick them.'

'They'll probably take them by surprise,' Hugh said.

'Surprise, ha!' Arna spat out at him. 'Not with a noisy loudspeaker like that, they won't. With all that food they'll be in the canteen for months, and we won't be able to have our sports display next week because school will have to close down.'

'Maybe Emma could surprise them,' Hugh said.

'Hey, where is Emma?' Phyllis said. 'She was here a minute ago.'

But Emma had darted down the shallow stairs ahead of her friends. Surprise was on her mind too. She crept along the wall of the quadrangle keeping to the bushes so that bossy teachers wouldn't see her and the robbers, who, after all, could be quite dangerous couldn't see her, until she was quite close to the canteen awning. She sat there a minute catching her breath. And then she whistled the bright clear whistle that would bring the birds from the sky.

They came swooping down in their tens and then their hundreds, great flocks of them settling into the quadrangle and all around the canteen, jostling each other for space.

'That'll make them chuck a wobbly, all right,' Emma said to herself. And it did!

The two desperadoes looked out of the canteen window and gulped in disbelief.

'I don't like this,' said the tall, thin one nervously screwing the lid back on the peanut butter jar tightly. 'Not one little bit.'

'I saw a film like this once, mate,' said the other robber uneasily. 'Birds kept coming out of the sky and it was gruesome.'

'Let's get out of here. Now. Before the birds attack,' the tall, thin one said, shuddering at the thought.

'The coppers are all out the front but I can see a back way,' the other robber pointed out. 'We can sneak out, go through the trees to the car, and head off. But what do we do with these heavy sacks?'

'Leave them for the birds,' the nervous one said, unlocking the canteen door and picking his way gingerly through the assembled birds. Beads of sweat broke out on his brow as he

saw more and more birds skimming in towards them. But the other one, who thought they'd gone through quite enough to get the money, threw the sacks over his shoulder before he, too, faced the birds.

The robbers scaled the wall with ease (even though one was weighed down by the money sacks) and headed for the car.

All this time Emma McDade was crouched in a bush by the wall listening to the robbers' escape plans. She crept away to the middle of the playground though the headmistress cried out to her, 'Emma McDade! Go home at once! There are bank robbers at large in the school, and no child's allowed here. And you can get rid of these birds. They're a hindrance to the law.'

And a police officer yelled at her, 'Clear off, little girl!'

But Emma began her whirling dance. Around and around she spun with her arms spread out and her face a white blur pointing up to the heavens. Of course the lightning flashed and the thunder boomed and the heavens opened in a fury.

In the thick blanket of rain no one could see Emma McDade any more. No one could see anything much. The robbers looked on the rain as providence.

'What a bit of luck,' said the nervous one to the other robber.

They sped through the trees and bush and down the lane and leapt into the waiting ALIANT even saying 'excuse me' to a cameraman who had his camera leaning on the bonnet.

The old ALIANT zoomed off down the road and the robbers probably would have escaped, but the freak storm that Emma had summoned was still raging and had sent torrents of water into the storm-water channel. The channel had overflowed, flooding the causeway at the end of the road.

'Drive through it, you idiot!' shouted the nervous one when his partner at the wheel slowed the ALIANT down to a crawl.

So he drove through it but the car was pulled this way and that by the seething waters. When a heavy old gum tree lurched and fell, the car finally plunged sideways off the causeway, sinking slowly down with the branches wedged across the doors. The robbers were trapped in the car and the waters were rising fast.

'Now what?' asked the one who had been driving.

'I think we should call — er, the police,' said the nervous one.

But they didn't need to. The cameraman had finally put two and two or rather one and one together, and, as the ALIANT sped off, realized that the two men who'd got into the car were the robbers. He told Officer MacDonald at once.

The police were quick to the scene of the submerging car. They called for the fire brigade and rescue equipment.

But Miss Myers, who could see the two robbers were only minutes away from drowning, said to Officer MacDonald, 'I think this is a job for McDade.'

'Is that a tow-truck service?' Officer MacDonald asked, putting down the two-way.

'Not exactly,' the Head said. 'But she'll get that car out of there quicker than any trucking service'.

'Well, let's not waste a moment. Get this McDade at once.'

And that was how Emma McDade in front of police officers and news reporters and television cameras and assorted others displayed her Samson-like strength to the whole world.

She tore the great heavy tree branches from the doors and lifted the car up and out of the raging channel, alone and unaided and to the utmost surprise of all those present who had not heard of her extraordinary power. There was a great cheer for young Emma as the two robbers emerged shivering and shaking. And another cheer when Officer Gilbert retrieved the two great sacks of money which were slightly damp now.

Then Hugh, who was terribly proud of Emma's brave action, told the reporters how Emma had also been responsible for the birds that had surprised the robbers out of hiding in the first place, and that Emma could bring them down out of the sky any old time.

'Wow, that's amazing! Quite amazing!' the reporter said so admiringly that Arna, who happened to be standing nearby, couldn't help but say, 'And that's not all she can do. No, sir, that's not all!'

Immediately a clutch of reporters closed in around Arna, and she found herself (though she'd been sworn to secrecy)

telling them that Emma had weather magic as well.

Then everyone closed in around Emma and she experienced the beginning of what was to quickly become a nightmare for herself and her parents and her immediate neighbours. She told them all about her magic powers and how she'd discovered them thinking they'd all go away. But they hadn't. The reporters clamoured after her and simply wouldn't leave her in peace, and when the whole world knew, it only got worse.

'They're still out there, great crowds of them,' Dad whispered, lifting the curtains just a smidgen to look out into the street.

'They've trampled our rock garden into the rock,' Mum said unhappily.

'And poor little Nia can't sleep a wink because of the noise and the lights out there. And she's cutting a new tooth, too,' said Emma unhappily. 'Phyllis's mother said Phyllis can't come over here to play any more. It's too hard getting through all the traffic.'

Emma McDade sat miserably through that evening with her parents. But the next morning she was her old self, bright and happy despite the noise still going on outside their house.

'I've decided to do something about all this,' she said to her mum and dad. 'I'm going to the United States to go on Good Morning America. Then I'll go on a world tour, especially of the hot countries.'

'But we don't want you to do all that unless you really want to,' they said.

'It means I'll miss the sports display and Nia's new tooth,' Emma sighed. 'But sometimes a girl's got to do what a girl's got to do.'

Dad put down his piece of toast and put his hand on his heart, 'If that's the way it's going to be, you know we'll support you wholeheartedly.'

'Of course,' said Mum, helping herself to more marmalade.

So Emma went out on to the front porch and told the crowd her plans. A great cheer went up.

'Show us your three magics, Emma McDade,' the crowd then implored.

'Okay,' she said, and she began her piercing whistle.

Everyone in the street gazed up expectantly, but instead of tens and hundreds of birds descending, one solitary bird came into sight, for a moment and then fluttered away again.

'Hold on,' Emma said quite puzzled, and she came out into the street and began her furious twirling. But not a cloud came into sight, and the sun continued to shine quite brilliantly.

'Hmm,' said Emma. 'You'll have to excuse me.' And she darted inside to her bedroom and her wardrobe. Though she heaved and pulled she couldn't budge the heavy old thing at all.

'I thought as much,' she said to herself, and then she called her parents. 'The magics have gone, all three of them. Completely.'

'Oh, wonderful,' they said. 'Now you don't have to go away, and you won't miss the sports display or Nia's tooth.'

So Mum and Dad went out to face the reporters and tell them the news. They were all gone in ten minutes: the cameras and lights and the tripods, all the trucks and cars and vans.

The street was so quiet that James and Charles came out to ride their skateboards at once.

When Phyllis came over to stay she asked, 'Will you miss your magic powers Emma?'

Mum always said you could adjust to anything in time, but Emma said, yes, she thought she might miss her magic powers. And she looked a bit sad.

That night Mum was looking for her opal ring. It had come from Lightning Ridge and had been her mother's before her.

Emma looked up from the kitchen table where she was playing Snakes and Ladders with Phyllis and said, 'It's in the kitchen sink drainpipe stuck in a piece of soap.'

'How could you possibly know it's there?' her mum asked crossly, still looking on the bench.

'Because I saw it there,' Emma said.

'Don't be ridiculous, you'd have to have Superman's X-ray vision to see it there!'

'Yep, it's there! I can see it! You'll have to unscrew the pipe at once.'

But Mum was standing stock still and staring hard at Emma. And then Emma stared at her and then Phyllis, and they all began laughing. They laughed and laughed and Dad came to see what the uproar was about.

'Just another magic, Mr McDade,' Phyllis explained. And when they told him that Emma had just developed X-ray vision, he laughed too.

'Well, I never,' he said.

And they knew there'd be no stopping the magics now.

Throughout her life for the years and years ahead (though she'd never know when or where or how) the extraordinary magics of Emma McDade would go on and on and on.

OXFORD UNIVERSITY PRESS

Oxford New York Toronto
Delhi Bombay Calcutta Madras Karachi
Petaling Jaya Singapore Hong Kong Tokyo
Nairobi Dar es Salaam Cape Town
Melbourne Auckland
and associated companies in
Berlin Ibadan

OXFORD is a trademark of Oxford University Press

National Library of Australia
Cataloguing-in-Publication data:

Hathorn, Libby.
The extraordinary magics of Emma McDade.

ISBN 0 19 554975 9.

I. Maya. II. Title.

A823'.3

Typeset by Bookset, Melbourne
Printed in Australia by Impact Printing, Melbourne
Published by Oxford University Press, 253 Normanby Road,
South Melbourne, Australia

*The Author gratefully acknowledges the support of the Literature Board of the
Australia Council, the Federal Government's Arts Funding and Advisory Board,
during the writing of this book.*